Why Is It Important to Exercise?

by Mrs. Matras' class
with Tony Stead

capstone classroom

When you exercise, even if it's just for a half hour a day, you are helping your body become strong and healthy. You will have more energy, and you'll live a longer, happier life! But some people don't exercise, and we want to convince them to be more active. Our class has been doing a lot of research about the benefits of exercise. In this book, we are going to tell you the many wonderful reasons for exercising and fun ways to get in a workout. Then you can decide—why is it important to exercise?

Exercise Keeps You Healthy

I believe that it is important to exercise. This is because exercising is good for your body. Another reason why exercising is important is because it helps your muscles grow. Exercise also keeps your body healthy.

You can exercise by running, walking, doing push-ups, doing sit-ups, and lifting weights. Did you know that exercising helps you lose weight? Did you also know that you really should exercise every day?

Running and walking are great ways to exercise, so get out today!

by Gerry

Why Exercise?

Some people might ask, "Why is it important to exercise?" Well, I have the answers to that question.

First, you need to exercise so you will be strong. Second, if you don't exercise, then you won't be in shape to run and play with somebody. Third, if you don't exercise, then you would just be sitting around on your couch, bed, or chair, watching TV or your DVD player or using the Internet. It's not good to spend so much time looking at screens.

For these reasons, I think it's important to exercise.

by Sophia

Exercise Is Important

Exercise is important. I'm going to give some reasons why you should exercise.

If you never exercise, you can turn into a lazy person and a couch potato. If you do exercise, your body and bones will get stronger.

If you don't work out, you're not going to be that strong. If you do work out, you'll be pretty strong. You can also stay in shape.

So please remember to exercise. Exercise helps keep you stronger and in shape.

by Matthew

100 Lbs
YAY I did It!!!
145 lbs

Exercise for 30 Minutes Each Day

I believe that you should exercise for at least 30 minutes each day. Exercise will help keep you healthy, and it is better than sitting in front of a TV watching shows or playing video games. There are many reasons why I believe this.

Exercise gets your heart pumping for good flow. But if you get sweaty, the liquids in your body come out, so you should be sure to drink plenty of water.

Exercise is also fun. You can go for a walk, jog, or run. These are a few things that adults may do. But did you know that playing is a form of exercise? You could go to the playground, swim, or play sports like basketball, baseball, or soccer. You could jump rope too.

Exercise also helps you stay fit and flexible. You might even be able to bend down and touch your toes!

Therefore, it's really important to exercise!

by Angelina

Exercise Keeps You Fit

I think exercise is a really good thing. It's great because it helps you stay in shape, have some muscles, and stay at a healthy weight. For example, you need to be healthy and strong to be good at wrestling. Exercise can help you become healthier and stronger.

Here are some examples of how to exercise: walk your dog, run around the block, and lastly, run or walk on a treadmill. But these are just a few ideas—you may come up with your own.

So keep working hard and keep exercising. It helps you stay in shape.

by Andrew

Exercise!

Exercising Is Fun!

It's important to exercise because it makes you healthy, it helps you get strong, it helps you grow, and it helps you live a better life because you are healthier. These are good enough reasons, but it's also a lot of fun!

A lot of people don't think that exercising can be enjoyable, but it is. You can take a walk. That's exercise. If you play sports, that's exercise. Playing outside with your friends is also exercising. Swimming in a swimming pool is exercising. Even if it's just for fun, playing at a park is exercising.

Remember, exercising helps you get strong and stay fit, but it's also a lot of fun!

by Kaylie

flames
flames
football Park
Pool
treadmill

Exercise Every Day

You need to exercise because then you will be healthier.

If you want to be healthy, then walk or run on a treadmill or jump on a trampoline. When you jump, you are exercising. When you walk and run, you are being healthy too.

Another reason why you should exercise is because you will be active and in shape. I think you should exercise every day because it helps you to stay healthy.

When you are exercising, it is important to drink water. So another brilliant thing to do is drink a lot of water while you walk or run or jump. Drinking water helps you exercise longer.

Exercising every day will help keep you healthy and strong. Exercising is important if you want to live a long life.

by Julia

Stronger, Faster, Better

You can exercise by running on a treadmill, doing push-ups, riding a bicycle, walking, jogging, running, and by doing many other activities. But why should you exercise? You should exercise for many reasons.

First, if you exercise, you can make your body stronger and faster. This will make you really, really happy. You will soon be able to park your car farther away from where you are going so that you can get even more exercise. Second, if you exercise, it can help your body digest your food. And finally, if you exercise, you can have a lot of fun.

As you can see, exercising is really important. It makes your body stronger and faster, it helps you digest food better, and it's a lot of fun.

by Sohan

Get Pumping for Exercise

I believe people should exercise because it helps keep them in shape and healthy. It's important to do, and if you like it, that's great. If you don't exercise, you can be unhealthy.

Maybe you're not sure where to go to exercise. If you're a kid, and you're not allowed to go to the gym, you can do many things at home and outside, like biking, running, walking, sit-ups, and push-ups. You can do a whole lot of things.

Exercise is also fun, and you can do it with a friend or sister or brother. It can also be fun because you can listen to music and that will get you pumping for exercise.

If you don't exercise, you may not be able to do a lot of stuff. Sports will help you exercise. That is what I do to exercise—I play sports: hockey, soccer, dance, football, and baseball.

For all of these reasons, I think that everyone needs to exercise!

by Allie

Having Fun and Exercising Too

Do you like to exercise? If you do, that's good! If you don't, that's bad. I will explain why I believe exercise is good.

Exercising is a thing we do all the time. So it seems we need to do it. Some examples of exercising are walking, running, jumping, and swimming. Even walking your pet or biking to your friend's house is exercising. There are different kinds of exercise, like cardio workouts and using machines, like a treadmill. Playing sports is also a good way to exercise.

Sports can trick you into exercising because you're having fun while playing them. Having fun is another reason why it's good to exercise. You just have to find a sport that you like.

Have you ever watched the Olympics? All the competitions the people do in the Olympics are a form of exercise. If you watch sports shows or the Olympics, you should pick out one or two sports that you think are fun and try them. If you like a sport, keep doing it because it's fun and good for you.

A final, big thing exercising does for us is that it helps us keep fit. Exercise will help you stay in shape.

So always remember to play sports to exercise. You'll have great fun while staying in shape!

by Natalie

The students in this class agree that exercise is very important for staying fit and healthy. Other benefits of exercising are that it's fun and helps you feel great. Now that you've read the students' arguments, do you agree that it is important to exercise? Why or why not? What arguments of your own would you add?